WORLDS

AWAY

Point of no return

Barry Kirkwood

Worlds Away
© Barry Kirkwood

National Library of Australia Cataloguing-in-Publication entry

Author: Kirkwood, Barry, author.

Title: Worlds away: point of no return / Barry Kirkwood.

ISBN: 9780992439002 (paperback)

Target Audience: For young adults.

Subjects: Science fiction.

Dewey Number: A823.4

Published with the assistance of www.loveofbooks.com.au

Chapter 1

Emerson hurriedly stumbles through the front door, peering through the dusty window, ensuring he hadn't been followed. Satisfied he's secure he pulls the green, musky curtains closed, leans up against the wall next to the window and examines the grimy, cheap motel room he had just entered. An empty side table sits on the eastern wall and above, an old television loosely hangs from its brackets. A dirty, brown mat leads into a tiny bathroom he had yet to encounter. Barely a double bed presses up against the opposite wall with a tired and battered bedside table struggling to hold up the phone. He lets out an exhausting sigh and lunges forward, slumping down onto the bed.

Emerson's thoughts wander back to his friend James. Still in disbelief, he places his hands over his head and attempts to snap himself out of the overwhelming emotion. He takes a look at his watch and is relieved to see he has six hours before Lana's show. As he falls, exhausted and restless onto the bed staring up at the cigarette-stained ceiling, Emerson thoughts retrace back to the memory of his father. How much he wished for his advice, his council, if just a single reassuring thought. Whether it was a conscious thought or the beginning of a dream, Emerson's mind slips back in time, to a simpler place. His old home town of Anamosa, Iowa. As his consciousness slips away, he falls off into an exhausted deep sleep.

▲▲▲

Emerson grew up an only child bought up by his father, John Ryles. His mother had sadly passed away giving birth to Emerson. John lived off the land as a grain farmer on the outskirts of the small country town of Anamosa, Iowa. He always modestly, but proudly, provided all he could for his only son. Emerson never went hungry, always made it to school and learned the true value of family and country. His father taught him about real America and the mid-west breathed life into his words. They lived on a beautiful farm surrounded by picturesque canyons scattered about the horizon. Many a sunset were spent with John and Emerson exploring the rugged giant walls of the canyons by air in John's two-seater crop duster. Emerson looked forward to those after school flights more than anything. As eager as he was to fly, at just 10 years old he wasn't quite old enough to manage the controls, but still marveled in the experience of flying as he watched every little turn, switch and gauge his father attended to.

John could see his son's future passion to be behind the controls. If ever there was a time that this was more true, it was one late Sunday afternoon while flying low through the canyons when, without warning, a deafening explosion erupted overhead, startling them both. Two military jets roared into view in a violent and frightening display of sheer gracefulness. Just as quickly as they appeared they vanished again into the distance. John and Emerson couldn't wipe the smile off their faces for a week to have seen such a sight.

Emerson's inspiration and determination to fly had been sealed from that moment on.

Emerson's local school was typical for a small country town with just over a hundred students. Always an inquisitive and intelligent boy, he was determined to do well in life and strived to make his father proud. Emerson mostly kept to himself at school never showing an interest to regular and common childish behavior. His upbringing taught him adult values early on and he respected his property and people he encountered, finding it easy to turn away when his peers would embark on a mission of misbehavior.

There was one classmate though that Emerson could always confide in, Lana Bailey. Lana and Emerson would become the closest of friends growing up; both would be in the same class all throughout middle school. Lana lived just a mile or so from the Ryles property with her grandparents, as her parents had unfortunately passed when she was just 6 in an accident with a truck just outside of Cedar Rapids.

The two were almost inseparable and spent many weekends exploring the surrounding rivers and farmland together. Some of their best times were spent hiking through the canyons sitting above one of the eastern facing peaks watching deer pick at the grasses and search for fallen berries. John was usually performing an afternoon dusting in the plane and would regularly give the kids a flyby and wave as he flew around.

Emerson and Lana seemed like they were never meant to be apart. Possibly this would have been the case if it wasn't for one fateful summers day. Emerson and Lana were now 14 and both were in class on a typical school day afternoon. All of a sudden, the classrooms silence was abruptly interrupted by the unmistakable sound of fire truck sirens ringing throughout their small town. As the sirens got louder and closer, the students rush to the window to watch the trucks rush by, quickly followed by two police cars also with lights flashing and sirens at full noise. An uneasy feeling falls over the classroom as confusion and tension came over the students. They watch with uncertainty as emergency services speed off into the distance. For a small town it was more often than not that someone everybody knew would require assistance, the hope was always that they were ok. They lived in a very tight nit and simple community that valued one another and any tragedy big or small was felt by all.

From one siren to another as the bell for the end of the day rang throughout the school. All the students quickly made their way outside to continue watching the various cars fly past, concerned to what had happened to draw such attention. Emerson was one of the first to make it outside, after looking around briefly for Lana he grows impatient and takes off up the road. It wasn't long before he draws closer to the farm, sirens ringing out breaking the usual silence of the countryside. More cars whizzed past him heading towards the commotion. Emerson begins to feel anxious the closer he gets. Growing more and more concerned to the direction the vehicles were going, he turns around to an oncoming blue pick-up truck that was heading to the scene. One of the occupants of the vehicle recognizes Emerson as he waves down the truck. The driver slows, he instructs Emerson to jump in the back with the others. He runs alongside of the pickup and is helped up by a couple of young men in the back who hoist him in.

As they get closer, smoke can be seen rising from the paddocks at the Ryle's property. They pull up to see the grain crop well alight, a swift blaze cutting though the field.

Several fire fighters and volunteers frantically try to contain the blaze which looked like it had been burning for a good hour, at least. Emerson watches anxiously as the men do whatever they can to stop the blaze from spreading towards the house. Choking smoke and flames fill the air as they fight to get the blaze under control. It's hard to make out anything and his father was nowhere to be seen. Emerson thinks his father must still be out dusting and may not even know what had happened. Eventually the fire becomes manageable and the last few sections are doused. The men can finally relax as they've saved the house at least. Just then a hand rests down on top of Emerson's shoulder. He turns around to see one of the police officers looking empathetically into Emerson's eyes. Another officer joins the first with a similar sad and disappointed look on his face. Emerson puzzled, turns back towards the burnt out crop as the smoke slowly clears. Debris and pieces of twisted metal begin to come into view, lying scattered throughout the field. His eyes follow the trail of metal until it stopped at the remaining pieces of the cockpit and engine. It was his father's crop duster. Emerson breaks away from the officer's grip and runs towards the remains of the plane. He's stopped by an ambulance officer as the fire crew is placing a white sheet over the cockpit. The ambulance officer convinces Emerson not to go over there. He takes him back to the two waiting police.

"I'm sorry son. He wouldn't have felt anything." says the officer.

Emerson's eyes stayed glued on the covered remains of his father's plane. He stayed with one of the officers as the emergency crews worked their way through the wreckage. Within the hour Lana and her grandparents arrived. Lana jumps out of the still moving car and comes running towards Emerson, throwing her arms around him and bursting into tears.

The two of them stand there not uttering a word, holding each other as the scene around them slowly dispersed.

That evening Emerson sat on the porch with Lana at the Bailey home, hand in hand. Mrs Bailey bought out a couple of glasses of lemonade as Mr Bailey was on the phone with the investigators. He hangs up the phone and motions to his wife to come inside. They tried to keep their voices low enough for the young couple not to hear, but Emerson still manages to catch most of it.

"That was the senior constable ... he said the investigators seem to think the crash was due to a broken linkage in the elevator controls. He never had a chance," Mr Bailey explained to his wife.

"Oh God ... this is horrible. Poor Emerson. What do we do now?"

"Well, I think we better put a call through to Emerson's relatives. I remember John saying his sister-in-law was the closest kin he had. In the morning we'll head over to the Ryles' farm and get her number."

"This is too much to believe," she cried as she turned her head to the young man sitting on the porch, now an orphan.

John's funeral was a moving send off. Emerson sat quietly with his Aunt and Uncle the whole time as one after the other, various friends and family from the town got up and recounted memorable and favorable tales about his father. It seemed like everyone had a memorable tale in John's memory. They respected and loved him very much throughout the community. Emerson stands at the edge of the casket as it's lowered into the grave, his father's airman badge in hand. At first he considers placing it into the grave but standing there he reminisced back to happier times flying around with his father and changes his mind. With tears in his eyes he pins the badge in the front right pocket of his jacket. Emerson swears from that moment on he would always strive to make his father proud.

After the service Emerson and Lana grew concerned to where he may now have to live, now having no family in Anamosa. Their fears unfortunately are realised later that evening when his Aunt regrettably breaks the news that Emerson would have to come back to Georgia with them. Being the closest kin, there was really no other choice. Emerson's Uncle parked up outside the Bailey farm as his Aunt hugs and says thank you and goodbye to Lana's grandparents. Lana and Emerson walk back up to the house emerging from the field after saying their own goodbyes. Lana walks up to the porch into her grandparents arms crying. Emerson seems shell-shocked, almost emotionless as everything becomes too much to take in.

The three of them get into the car as they make their way to the airport. Emerson looks back at Lana as they drive away, he watches her into the distance helpless as her grandparents console her. At that time Emerson wondered if he would ever see Lana again, strangely somehow through all the grief he felt a glimmer of hope; that this wasn't the last time he would set eyes on Lana Bailey.

Chapter 2

Emerson settled into his new home in Brookhaven, Georgia, relatively well. Despite the loss of both his father and Lana he seemed to have kept himself together. His Aunt and Uncle were supportive in whatever he wanted to head towards and it wasn't long before Emerson made those intentions clear.

"Airforce? Are you serious?" Emerson's Aunty queried.

"It's all I've ever wanted," he responded.

"It's just... your father... "

"I know and it should stop me from wanting to fly but all it's done is convince me even more."

"You know Liz, it's what John would've wanted for the boy," chimed in Emerson's Uncle.

There was an intense moment of silence as Emerson's Aunt Liz contemplated the wishes of her late brother-in-law. She looked from her husband to Emerson and with a smile, outstretched her arms to him. He replied in kind and they hugged.

"I'll tell you what. You pass everything at school and we'll sign off on it ok? I mean everything though."

Emerson agrees; as if they had a chance of changing his mind. "Not a problem. I have to have the best grades to even be close to being accepted."

Sure enough, Emerson lives up to his promise and excelled at High School. He passed every subject with ease and in his final year was even awarded valedictorian for his graduation.

Much like his earlier years, back in Anamosa where he kept to himself, Emerson didn't spend much time mixing with the school crowd. When he wasn't studying, he was logging flying hours at a local flight school. One of the greatest things about Brookhaven was the choice of flying schools available to him. He found serenity in the air and it was where he felt most connected to his father. By the time he had graduated, Emerson had logged over 80 hours flying time and was even encouraged to consider becoming a commercial pilot.

However, the encouragement couldn't sway his desire to be in the military. It seemed a fitting tribute to his father and the adrenalin involved in being a commercial pilot just didn't come close to what the air force offered.

Straight out of High School, at 18 years old, Emerson was accepted into the US Air Force Academy in Colorado. Emerson adjusted well to the rigid schedule and demands asked of the cadets and he continued to excel at all he put his heart and mind into.

For the first time since Lana, Emerson found friendship with some of his peers. Three other eager cadets and Emerson made up a four man squad that began to form a close bond through basic training, test flight missions and also on a social level. Ben and Chris were incredibly outgoing and social guys. They lived freely and thrived off the rush that flying offered. They could also cut loose with the best as they quickly built a reputation of being the party boys of the squad. They built a rebellious-type bond between each other, swinging into 'wing-man' mode for one another at a moment's notice. James, on the other hand, was the more mature one of the group, the leader who always managed to steer them away from serious trouble when out and about, breaking free of the regimental life on base. Emerson often found himself confiding in James and a mutual respect and understanding was built between them.

Several months into their training the boys were well on their way to becoming fully-fledged military pilots, getting the occasional taste of R&R along the way. The big wide world and all it offered was before them, they could barely contain their enthusiasm and anticipation, especially Ben and Chris. There was no denying that they all worked tremendously hard and were committed to their careers in the military, but as young men do, at any chance they could, they'd all cut loose and many alcohol induced nights would ensue.

One night, only months away from their graduation as pilots, they went into the city for a few hours of downtime. They were still in uniform after just completing a series of theory exams so James ensured they all agreed to behave. However, like a scene from Top Gun, James and Emerson would watch their comrade's meager attempts to woo women. They often succeeded but the most entertaining part was the actual lead-up. Ben spotted four ladies across the bar and caught their eye.

"Ok boys, I'm up. Fifty dollars, I'll have all four of them here in less than 3 minutes."

"You're on." Chris laughs, pulling a fifty dollar note from his wallet. "Two maybe, but all four... not a chance Benny."

James sarcastically agreed, "As much as I would like some womanly company tonight, I could do with some more green in my jeans. No chance Ben."

He slaps another $50 on top of Ben's. By this stage Emerson had already withdrawn his cash and laughs as he throws it over with the rest of the cash.

"Thanks boys, $150 in my pocket."

They laughed as Ben greasily walks over towards the women. He reaches them and with a smile begins his pitch.

"And 3 minutes counting…" Chris joked.

It wouldn't have even taken 90 seconds and Ben was leading all four ladies over to the table. He secretly motioned with his fingers for the men to pay up; all the boys could do was shake their heads in disbelief.

Introductions were made and Ben offered the ladies drinks using his new found winnings. While waiting at the bar for the drinks, Chris joined him to help carry them over.

"What the hell did you say to those girls Ben? That was impressive." Chris asked in awe.

Ben proceeded to relay his sales pitch with fake sincerity; "I just said we were flying out tomorrow on a dangerous mission. That it was possible we might not return and that our final desire was for us all to have one final drink each with a beautiful woman before flying to our possible deaths."

Chris laughed so hard the rest of the table turned to see what the commotion was.

"I can't tell you all my secrets", Ben smiled in reply.

Chris shakes his head at Ben's arrogance and carries the drinks to the table. The four men and women trade shots for a while, and Ben and Chris marveled in the attention of the gorgeous young women as always.

It wasn't uncommon for Emerson to often think back to Lana, what could have been, where or how she was. Almost 10 years had passed since he watched her standing on the Bailey's porch while driving off that fateful day. James knew better than anyone the constant emptiness and hurt Emerson would regularly feel. He could see he wasn't into the night's antics as much as the others. As time had gone on since Emerson's father's death, it seemed more and more unlikely he would ever see Lana again. He finished his drink and excused himself.

"Back soon, going to duck out for a bit," Emerson said and wandered outside for some air. He stood outside the bar and watched the passerby's, reflecting on what could have been if he had stayed in Anamosa or at least, went back to visit.

"You ok?" James had come out to check on his wing man.

"Yeah fine, just getting some air."

"Ben and Chris seem to have struck a home run," James says, indicating they'd done well with their new dates.

"Not surprising," Emerson replied with a strained smile, "I might call it a night I think. The boys look like they've got it under control."

"Yeah, those girls aren't quite up to the conversation, if you know what I'm saying," James laughed, "I'll join ya, we'll shoot over there for a coffee and head back to base, yeah?"

James points to the diner across the street as they finish their drinks and head over to say their farewells to the ladies, leaving Chris and Ben to work their magic.

'Double trouble now, no doubt the next morning would be full of entertaining stories,' Emerson thought as they headed over to the diner.

"Black, no sugar thanks," Emerson orders, standing at the counter sorting his change.

"And you love?" the waitress asked James.

"Ah, yeah, the same thanks and this," James picks up the daily paper from the rack

and slides the correct change for the coffee's and paper onto the counter.

They both sit down by the window as the waitress brings over two cups and a pot of fresh coffee.

"Thanks darlin'," James replies, then splits the newspaper in two. "You want?" He asked offering the front half to Emerson.

"Nah, I'm good." Emerson declines.

James begins reading as they drink their coffee. Emerson takes a sip, and then notices something on the back of James' paper, nearly spitting his coffee across the room. He grabs the back section of the paper quickly off James.

"Holy shit, I don't believe it!" exclaimed Emerson.

"What the hell?" James responded in shock.

"I know this girl." Emerson replies, pointing at a beautiful, young woman's photo highlighted in an advert in the top corner of the paper.

Lana had always loved to sing as they were growing up. She had a great passion for songwriting that came from the heart. He had always told her she could do anything and that

singing could be her ticket out of their small town. He knew she had an amazing, sultry voice, but never had of thought in a million years he'd be so lucky to see her name and photo in the local paper advertising a public performance. Even better was that it was happening at a local bar, which was close to the base, in just two days time! As he reads each line a euphoric relief washed over him. After ten years, right in front of him, a photo of his childhood sweetheart all grown up and coming to town. Familiar feelings of a time long ago come flooding back. Like fate had reached out and finally given Emerson a helping hand, there was no way he was going to miss this.

He proceeded to explain who Lana was to James and showed him the concert date.

"Mate, we can't get out of base at such short notice. We booked tonight out two weeks ago and nearly missed out. Plus we already have five days R&R booked in for next week."

"I can't miss this James." Emerson firmly stated.

The only option he had was to go AWOL. Not usually one to break the rules, the decision came easily enough as feelings and regrets of the past played on his mind. James supported his brother and agreed to keep the secret of Emerson sneaking off the base for the night. Although he hadn't tried it before, Emerson felt confident he could get away with it. The thought of seeing Lana again outweighed any obstacle. It was going to happen, no matter what.

Chapter 3

Two days on base passed quickly. Emerson waited until dusk to make his 'get-away' from camp. Lana's concert started at 1900hrs and there was at least a three mile hike cross-country to avoid being spotted. He waited until just after dusk and headed to the barracks door. He quietly opened it a couple of inches right on time to see James walk past heading towards the base gates.

It was simple; as long as James could keep the gate guard distracted for about two minutes, it would give Emerson just enough time to leave the barracks and get to the motor pool exit, out of sight from the MPs. It worked like clockwork. Shortly after James had sent the Corporal through the morning reports, he caught a glimpse of Emerson making it out of the motor pool exit, on his way to Lana.

"Never mind Corporal."

"Sir?"

"It can wait... as you were."

With that James heads back to the mess hall with a sly grin on his face thinking of his best mate running off into the night to find his girl.

Emerson stayed off the road the entire time, fearful of an officer spotting him. Just a few months from getting his wings, the last thing he needed was to put that in jeopardy, but for once his heart led before his head.

It was right on 1900hrs when the bar came into view. Emerson checked his watch then put on a light jog to the entrance. He pays the cover charge at the door and enters the bar. Once inside he was mindful to continue keeping a low profile and scanned the room. It was an average sized venue filled with around 80 people. He spotted no-one he knew but decided not to risk being seen and quickly grabbed a drink and found a stool at the back of the room. At least if someone from the base came in, he would see them first and have a chance to remain unrecognized.

Just then the MC headed towards the microphone standing in the center of the stage. Behind him was a pianist, drummer and a bass player, all of which became quite obscure as the house lights dimmed and a spotlight shone on the MC. After 10 long years, and coming to the conclusion he would never see Lana again, Emerson anxiously waited, the moment he had wished for, for so long.

"Ladies and Gentlemen, tonight we have a beautiful talented up and coming young artist, guaranteed to leave you breathless. Not only with her beauty but her magnificent, spell bounding voice. All the way from the gorgeous mid-west, The Bluehorn Restaurant and Bar proudly presents Lana Bailey!'

There was a modest clap and cheer from the audience as the spotlight went out on the MC. For Emerson, the hustling of the patrons and clinking of the glasses muffled into nothing as he zoned out into the stage in anticipation. With a flash, the spotlight came back onto the stage and standing within it was the most beautiful, elegant woman Emerson had ever seen. That young vulnerable girl was no more. Her long black hair perfectly overshadowing half of her face while the other half glowed within the light. Her porcelain skin shining in brilliance as the musicians slowly began to come to life. Lana lifted her head to sing, shivers ran through Emerson's body as her sultry voice swept him back in time. Her body was shaped wonderfully in the tight, long, black evening dress with a modest split up the left side. As her soulful voice and lyrics of love and sadness embraced and entertained the audience, Emerson sat there enthralled with the performance and feeling immense pride over the beautiful and successful young woman Lana had now become.

Back at base, things were not panning out as hoped for James or Emerson. His disappearance, unfortunately, had not gone unnoticed.

"I understand a friend of Cadet Ryles had arrived last minute in town Major," James was attempting to smooth the effect Emerson's AWOL had caused, but it wasn't working.

"I don't give a God-damn rat's ass why he is where he is Senior Cadet. I just want to know where the hell he is! Do you understand me?!"

"Yes Sir!" James replied.

There is an airy silence as the Major awaits a more defined response from James.

"Well... ?!" requested the Major.

"Sir?"

Losing his patience, the Major slams his fists onto the desk, "You have 3 seconds to tell me where the hell Cadet Ryles is before you, him and your whole entire God-damn squad are thrown in the brig. 1... 2... "

"I think he may be at that local bar in town, The Bull Horn? Sir." James, quickly divulged.

"The Blue Horn," The Major corrected.

"Sir?"

"The BLUE Horn, BLUE Horn, not the Bull Horn!" he calls out to the two sergeants outside his office door, "Sergeant! Take this man back to his barracks."

Emerson had hardly moved throughout the whole performance. He barely touched his drink, as Lana's voice and lyrics captivated and spellbound the entire audience. He was purposely to far back in the room for Lana to have noticed him and he didn't think that was a bad thing. Just as the crowd gave a standing ovation and cheered, Emerson's received a message on his phone in his pocket. He ceases clapping and reads a text from James.

'Couldn't cover with the Major. MP's on their way.'

Emerson looked back up to the stage. The house lights had come on and Lana was off stage. *'I have time,'* he thinks to himself. He finishes his drink and heads up to the bar for a second. It wasn't too long before Lana came out to meet and mingle with the public. Emerson watched with awe as she owned the room. He waited until she had got herself comfortable before deciding to approach her. She was sitting at the far end of the bar with a spritzer chatting with the pianist. Thoughts of whether she would even remember him began to creep into his mind, it had been so long, what felt like a life time ago. But with the MP's due any minute, it was now or never. He walks up behind her while motioning to the barman for another drink. Lana is mid-conversation with her band mate when she pauses at the sound of a familiar voice.

"You always had a great voice," Emerson comments.

Lana turns and with a look of disbelief, locks eyes with her old childhood sweetheart, her lost best friend. Without uttering a word, she stands and instantly wraps her arms around him in delight.

"You were amazing up there," repeated Emerson.

Lana breaks the hug and stuttering, introduces him to the pianist and vice versa. She stands there glowing at the sight of Emerson and her joyfulness fills him with comfort.

They had barely said two words to each other before Emerson notices two MP's walk through the front doors of the bar. He sees them spot him and drops his head in disbelief. Lana can't help but notice the change in his demeanor.

"What's wrong?" she asks.

"How long are you in town for?" he quickly replies.

"Just until tomorrow, We leave for a tour of California."

"I had to go AWOL to see you tonight. This happened so fast, I didn't have a choice. Our squad will be on leave next week. I'll find you again, I promise."

He quickly scribbles his number onto a napkin and manages to hand it to her before the MP's acknowledge Emerson, placing a hand on his shoulder.

"Cadet Ryles. I'm going to have to ask you to come with us."

Emerson begrudgingly accepts the MP's request, as they muscle-up, standing either side of him. Emerson looks back and gives Lana a comforting smile as the three men exit the bar. Lana is still in a state of shock, but delighted at the same time as she realizes she's clutching her childhood sweetheart's number. A moment she had dreamed about for many years, but thought would never come.

Chapter 4

It seemed like an eternity as James and Emerson waited in their barracks for the Major. By association, Ben and Chris had also been drawn into Emerson's exertion. They entered the barracks 20 minutes after Emerson was bought back and told to wait with them. Emerson explained what he had done, which both Ben and Chris found immensely hilarious and congratulated him for breaking the rules.

Finally, the men were summoned to the briefing room where both Major Daniels and Captain Adams were waiting. Both had stern, unmoving expressions and grimaced as the four entered the room. They all saluted upon entry.

"At ease Gentlemen," Captain Adams quietly instructed.

"We have strict guidelines in the military," began the Major, "Guidelines that need to be adhered to otherwise there is chaos."

"Yes sir!" replied the four cadets in unison.

"Shut up!" exclaimed the Major, "If we were called to war, do you think it is acceptable to be busy chasing a piece of ass while your country is being invaded? Is that more of a priority than doing your sworn duty?"

"No sir!" replied the cadets, again in unison.

"Shut up!" repeated the Major.

"It appears only one of you is actually guilty of being AWOL. Cadet Mason, you were aware that Cadet Ryles had left the base?" asked Captain Adams.

"Yes sir," replied James.

"And you chose not to report it?"

"No sir, I did not."

"Why is that Cadet?"

"Loyalty. Captain. Ryles is my brother in arms sir. My wingman. I need to have his back at all times and vice versa, sir," James replied confidently.

Both the Major and Captain looked at each other, contemplating his supporting, yet misguided words.

"Very well Cadet. While I admire your loyalty and commitment with your fellow cadet, there needs to be the same loyalty and commitment shown to the base, to the force. Consider yourself lucky you walk with a warning. Dismissed."

The four men surprised, saluted and turned to walk away.

"Ryles. You stay," demanded the Major.

James looked at Emerson who nodded acceptance and motioned for them to leave. James closed the door behind him as Emerson turned back to face his superiors. At that moment Lana entered his mind. A vision of her on that stage. He smiled.

"Do you find this amusing Cadet?" asked the Major.

"No sir. Sorry sir."

"Sit down Emerson," asked the Captain.

Emerson was surprised to hear him use his first name but tentatively took a seat. Captain Adams opened a manila folder. Emerson presumed it was his file. As the

Captain skimmed through the file, the Major walked over to the coffee machine and poured himself a cup.

"I find it hard to believe this was an error of judgment Emerson," began the Captain, "You are a leader. Your stats show some of the most impressive results the air force has seen in some time. Your commitment to your wings is second to none and you're respected by your peers, as is Cadet James Mason. To date your behavior, professionalism and performance is at the top of the squad results."

"Ah, thank you sir," commented a tentative Emerson.

"I read your file earlier. Your father, your history. I understand the person you visited tonight was tied to this in some way."

"Yes sir. She was. She is," responded Emerson, looking down at the table.

The Captain stood up and closed the file. His tone changed and a more definitive voice came through;

"The air force is nothing unless it has its brotherhood. In this age we need to show support and solidarity in times that test us. Do you agree Cadet?"

"Yes, yes I do sir," replied Emerson standing at attention.

"This incident will not be recorded on your file. We have decided a verbal warning is enough. I know you don't see this as a free pass..." stated the Captain before Major Daniels interrupted;

"And we know this won't happen again,"

"No Sir!" exclaimed Emerson.

"So, we will leave it here. Your leave for this week is still granted. Make sure you and your four cohorts come back revitalized. The squad graduates very soon. One of the best we have. You will be leading graduation. Understand?" stated the Captain.

"Yes sir. Thank you sir, sirs. I'm proud to be the pilot you both believe I am. I will not let the force down."

Both the Major and Captain nod in agreement and head towards the door. The Major still has a relatively stern look on his face. Captain Adams stops and puts his hand on Emerson's shoulder.

"We know Cadet. We know."

Waiting outside Ben, Chris and James eagerly waited. Emerson appeared with a somber look on his face giving the others cause for disappointment. He looked up at them and a sly smile appeared.

"California, here we come!" exclaimed Emerson.

The boys embraced with solidarity and cheered with excitement.

"What did they say?" asked James.

"This won't be happening again. They have kept it off my record and written the whole thing off," Emerson replied.

"You lucky bastard," congratulated Ben slapping him on the shoulder.

"Well, let's start getting things together. Last time as cadet's boys. Let's set it off!"

With that, the boys headed back to the barracks in preparation for their final R&R prior to becoming fully-fledged pilots.

Chapter 5

The next five days leading up to their R&R went by fairly quickly. Emerson and Lana talked constantly on the phone every night, catching up and making plans to meet in California. In their fatigues, the four cadets finally arrived at their hotel in Santa Barbra. They were excellently located, right on the beach front and within walking distance of all the bars and clubs. As they unloaded the jeep, Chris couldn't help but take notice of the various bikini-clad beauties in all directions.

"Boys, she's gonna be a long night," he laughed.

The others admired the view and joined him in jubilated laughter, then proceeded to check into the hotel. As the others got changed into more casual attire, Emerson sent a text through to Lana.

'We made it, just checking in. See you tonight. Can't wait.'

He smiled and looked out the window at the sun-kissed sand and took a moment to enjoy the elation he was feeling. James joined him in his view and then patting him on the back, motioned for them to leave.

"Let's go brother. She's waiting for you."

Emerson smiled at James and excitedly returned the brotherly back-pat.

"All right boys. First rounds on me."

The cadets relaxed at the first beach front bar they found. One hour in and Ben and Chris had already struck up a conversation with two stunningly, beautiful blondes. James was relaxing with a Corona talking to his family on his cellphone. Emerson was smiling as he watched and enjoyed seeing his friends relaxing. He swung his stool around to get a better look at the beach and like a scene from a romance novel, out of the back of a beautiful black Cadillac stepped Lana. It was as though the world slowed to a snail's pace as she stood gracefully, allowing the breeze from the ocean to sweep through her gorgeous dark hair. A tight dark one piece dress clung to her beautifully shaped body as she turned to the driver thanking him. The Cadillac drove away leaving the most stunning sight Emerson had ever seen. The backdrop of the beach and crashing waves helped exaggerate the beauty that was Lana.

He stood and walked towards the front of the bar as she made her way towards him. There was an airy silence as they stood less than two feet from each other. Without a word said, they embraced and locked lips for the first time. It was hard to believe it had taken so long for them to be so close and Emerson could feel the comfort and belonging he always had in her company. Their romantic embrace came to an end at the sound of wolf whistles and cheers from Ben and Chris, who by this time had joined James in watching the reunion of Lana and Emerson. Emerson grinned and guided Lana towards his buddies, introducing them and then offering her a drink.

Emerson and Lana hit it off as thought they had never been apart. As they caught each other up on the past ten years, a slight sadness between the two of them was felt as they realised they had spent so much time apart. Sadness soon turned to jubilation. They stared into each other's eyes with such childlike excitement as the reality of them being together again sunk in.

The drinks kept coming and the music got louder, the good times continued to roll on and the five of them danced the night away. Eventually James, Chris and Ben each found the company of a sultry lady of the beach and the group broke away to their own personal pieces of heaven. Inseparable, Emerson and Lana eventually made their way onto the beach. Walking along the sand barefoot with the lights of Santa Barbra on one side and the moonlight reflecting of the whitewash on the other, Lana stopped walking and pulled Emerson towards her.

"I never stopped thinking of you. Loving you," she openly shared.

Emerson slowly guided her hair from her face and placed it behind her ear. He gazed at her face with awe and admiration as she looked at him with intense love and emotion.

"I know, I think I have always known. You were never far from my thoughts. I thought I had lost you forever."

"I'm so proud of you. Your Dad would be proud too, you know that, don't you Emerson?" she confidently asked.

Emerson nodded. Lana guided his face down to hers and softly began kissing his lips, his cheek, his neck and before long the two of them had collapsed onto the sand and began making love. They remained in that secluded spot, oblivious to the world, for the rest of the night.

The following three days continued to be a combination of partying, beach combing, relaxation and women for all four cadets, but in Emerson's case it was just the one woman; his woman. Sitting at the Rosalie Café on the third day, Emerson receives a phone call from their Commanding General.

After speaking briefly he ends the conversation: "Yes sir.... We're leaving now. We'll be there ASAP," Emerson stated and ended the call. "Looks like we're heading back early boys... We have to be at Moody AFB, Georgia by 1800hrs tonight."

"You're freakin' joking" Chris exclaimed in haste.

"Afraid not," replied Emerson.

"Did they say what for?" James replied

"He didn't say, but apparently there's four F-18s fueled up and waiting for us at Vandenberg," Emerson replied disappointedly.

The mood completely changed as the four cadets stood up and collected their belongings ready to head back to the hotel and pack.

Emerson turns to Lana, saddened to say goodbye. James stops him before he utters a word.

"Stay here brother. I'll get your stuff together and we'll meet you out front of the hotel in 20, OK?" James offered.

Emerson thanked him and James, with a soft wave and smile, left Lana and Emerson to it.

"It's not enough," exclaimed Lana, disappointed by the thought of him leaving.

Emerson took her by the hand and pulled her into him.

"What? You think I'm going to let you go now? After ten years? The world's too small for us to be apart. This is just the beginning. I'll never be far away."

He sensitively kissed her before breaking into a more passionate showing. The old lady in the seat next to their table forcefully cleared her throat as to express her distaste. Lana and Emerson smiled at her then laughed to one another, before slowly heading back to the hotel.

Lana had decided to give them all a ride to the airport and arranged her driver to pick them up and take them to Vandenberg Air Force Base, where they would fly back to their requested destination at Moody AFB in Georgia.

Ben, Chris and James all hugged and kissed Lana goodbye, expressing their delight in meeting her. Emerson and Lana embraced and passionately kissed one more time before saying their temporary goodbyes. She watched as the four men suited up and proceeded to the main hanger where there planes were waiting. Emerson climbs up into the cockpit and gives Lana a final wave and smile goodbye, before pulling the canopy down and firing up the engine.

Lana returns the smile and wave and watches as the series of F-18s take off, roaring into the distance. Feelings of euphoria and happiness wash over her as the missing part of her life had finally been returned. She acknowledged he had left, but warmed to the thought that this time it was only temporary. Before she knew it, Emerson would be back in her arms again.

chapter 6

After a couple of hours flying, reflecting on a great getaway and exciting new chapter in Emerson's life, he and the squadron touched down at Moody Air Force Base where they were immediately ushered into the central briefing room. Waiting for them deep in conference was Captain Adams and two other commanding Generals they'd never seen or heard of before. The Generals have a very persuasive yet no nonsense persona about them. Major Daniels comes into the room and walks past the full squad, scanning them up and down as he passed. He instructs them to take a seat. Emerson, James, Chris and Ben are intrigued with what news could be so important as to cut their R&R short. The Major hands a file to the Captain who relays something to both Generals before they all turn to face the squad. The taller of the two Generals, and the one with the most stars on his shoulder, steps forward and engages the squad.

"Good evening cadets. I am pleased to be here today and pass this mission onto Captain Adams. It is a highly classified mission and has great importance to national security. Understand this is the final stage to your training. All cadets need to undertake a mission of this nature as a test for them to adapt to the real pressure of dealing with classified missions for the United States Air Force. Captain Adams has informed me that I am looking at some of the best damn pilots he has ever seen, so my confidence is high."

Being the first mission of this kind for the cadets, a sense of achievement and eagerness stirred amongst the group. The two Generals wished the cadets good luck, saluted the squad and the Captain before exiting the room, leaving Captain Adams to go through the specifics of the mission.

"The mission itself is reasonably straight forward. Two members of the squad are required to fly a loaded cargo plane, escorted by two armed fighters, to an undisclosed location. The armed fighters will also be manned by cadets of this squad," the Captain began.

They continued to go through the details of the route, altitude, speeds, etc. As the Captain didn't want to isolate any one cadet as better than the other, he opened the decision making process of who was to be undertaking which task to a simple game of chance. He presented a handful of straws and each cadet took one. Chris and Emerson both come up short, regrettably getting the pleasure and responsibility of flying the C-5 Galaxy cargo plane. Ben and James were to pilot the F-18 fighters as escorts.

Early in the morning the following day, the cadets are given a final briefing on the mission before making their way to the hangers. It was just on 4am when the men arrived at the aircrafts fully prepared and ready to fly. Chris and Emerson step up onto the loading ramp of the cargo plane, closing the massive cargo bay door behind them. Expecting to see a fully loaded plane, they were surprised as to what they saw. Their precious cargo is sitting ominously at the front of the bulk head standing over seven feet tall, rectangular in shape with a base the size of a small car. The two cadets were puzzled to what it could possibly be. Emerson approached the object for further inspection. It was some kind of device with solid black tinted glass encased in a cast steel boxed frame. Emerson placed his hand on the device, suddenly pulling away, discovering it was freezing cold to touch. Emerson and Chris looked at each other realizing that only speculation could fill their thoughts to what it might be and knew their focus was to be on the mission. They made their way to the cockpit and thought no more of it as they prepared the plane for take-off.

The sounds of the planes massive turbine engines begin to wind up, as the three planes begin to taxi down the runway. Emerson made one final check before he pushed the throttles wide open. The planes massive bulk begins creeping down the runway faster and faster, three hundred & forty thousand pounds of American Airforce muscle hurtling down the seemingly endless stretch of tarmac. Emerson pulls back on the column as the front wheels begin lifting off the ground, finally they're in the air. Within seconds later, Ben and James take off in the F-18's. Remaining in close proximity and in formation, the three planes climbed to 30,000 feet. They settled into their flight plan heading north-west and awaited further instruction from the ground as to their exact destination.

Three hours into the flight, continuing on their scheduled path, Emerson receives a radio transmission, as planned, of the exact destination. He entered the coordinates into the computer and Chris corresponded with the planes navigational system which was redirecting them north. Emerson radios through to Ben and James.

"Eiffel 9 6 to Echo 12, Echo 9. Course laid in B9 9 6 2 38^0 E6 2 2 1 22^0 North-North-West. Acknowledge."

"Echo 12 Acknowledged Alpha 9 6. Sharp right turn, on your mark." James replied from his fighter.

"Echo 9 Acknowledged." Ben responded.

Emerson begins to pitch the cargo plane into a steep sweeping bend, "And mark."

Slowly all 222 feet of the C-5 Galaxy massive wingspan tilts almost vertically as Emerson banks the plane into a hard right-hand turn. The two men admire the planes maneuverability as Emerson holds the plane pitched hard right when suddenly, a loud snapping noise resonates thought the cabin followed by a shuddering crash. The cargo dislodged from its position and slid across the floor smashing up against the sides of the plane. Emerson and Chris look at one and other with concern as Emerson levels out and continues on the scheduled course. Chris unbuckles himself and heads back to the cargo hold to inspect the situation and try and re-secure the cargo. No training or preparation could have helped Chris for what he was about to witness. The blackened tinted window encasing the cargo lay smashed to pieces, scattered along the cargo hold floor. As Chris edges closer, a heavy mist of dissolving liquid nitrogen flowed freely from the compromised vessel. Chris edged closer to inspect the extent of the damage. Peering in through what was left of the compromised tinted glass, Chris fell back in fright. He was stunned with what he saw, terrified in fact. He crouched down in silence with his hand over his mouth, trying to remove what he had seen from his mind but it was etched there for good now. He tried to gather his thoughts and slowly headed back to the cockpit.

"What's the status?" Emerson asked.

At first there was no reply. Emerson turned to his co-pilot who was stunned, shocked, terrified and confused.

After a moment Emerson asked again, impatiently, "Chris, what the hell is it?!"

Chris managed to snap out of his trance-like state long enough to reply, "You wouldn't believe what is back there."

Realizing he was getting nothing out of Chris, Emerson switched the central controls to auto and unbuckled himself from his seat. He made his way back to the cargo hold to inspect the situation for himself. The cargo still lay toppled over while the eerie mist continued to seep out of the compromised containment hold. Emerson leant forward and peered into the object through the shattered glass but the mist was obstructing his full field of view. He catches a glimpse of an outline of what looked to be an obscure-looking, long arm. As he goes in for a better look, Chris suddenly interrupts, "Emerson!!!! You need to get back here. There's something coming up on us fast, heading right this way. It's fast, shit. It's really fast."

Emerson quickly gets himself back into his seat and reset the controls to manual. He spots the object closing in on radar. Slight panic and confusion set in as they both confirm the unidentified object moving unordinary fast in their direction.

"How fast is it going? That can't be right."

"Off the measure, At least mach 5 and closing in."

Emerson switched his communications back to the F-18's.

"Eiffel 9 6 to Echo 12, Echo 9. Verify bogey closing in from behind. Acknowledge."

Silence.

"Eiffel 9 6 to Echo 12, Echo 9. Verify unidentified bogey closing in fast 105 degrees East. Acknowledge."

Emerson tries resetting his comm setting to re-establish communication with Ben and James. As the object closes in, suddenly the radar screen begins to flicker and static comes over the radio. Chris begins flicking through channels only to get the same response each time. Now without communication and radar, they were flying blind. Emerson realized the object should have hit or passed them by now. He peered out to his left to see James' F-18 holding position. Chris confirmed the same for Ben out on the right. The two fighters off each wing seemed completely oblivious as to what was unfolding. Looking forward out over the front of the carrier, Emerson tries to get a visual on the object, as it should have passed or impacted by now. Just as he looks up, he catches a glimpse of an ominous black craft hovering directly above them. Before he has time to react, an immense blinding white light floods the cockpit. Both men throw their hands up, shielding themselves from the glare. The two men become transfixed, frozen from the light, looking at each other searching for some kind of explanation. Emerson tried to move but it was as though the light had a physical grasp on him. Chris' eyes slowly begin to adjust and make out shapes through the stunning light. Just as he makes shape of Emerson, right in front of his eyes Chris watched as Emerson literally dissolves and particularized, disappearing into thin air. Chris can't believe his eyes as he now finds himself completely alone. Suddenly he feels the intense light transfix on him holding him down, heavily frozen in time.

James and Ben are both oblivious to the unfolding situation just yards away from them. Still struggling to understand why they'd suddenly lost radar and coms. They hadn't seen any light at all and were yet to notice the black ominous object hovering over the cargo plane. James is the first to spot the UFO, his heart pounding out of his chest. A craft of another world, right there, not fifty yards from his right wing. He quickly loops his jet around and positions the fighter into attack position, Ben follows suit shortly after. Both pilots frantically try to make contact over the radio but deafening static fills all channels as panic and confusion set in.

James could see the light shooting down into the cockpit of the cargo plane. He takes aim at the UFO and fires a single missile.

Chris instantly feels the grasp of the light release its grip from him, falling back into his seat. It all happens as though in slow motion.

As Chris' field of vision returns he looks out over the front of the plane to see the huge black agile craft sweep down in front of the cockpit. Time stood still as the craft was so close he could literally make out the alien detail of the vessel as it shot downwards in an evasive maneuver to avoid the F-18's missile. The missile is locked onto the UFO and turns sharply downwards to pursue the craft. Chris can only watch helplessly as he sees the craft swoop down and out of view. The missile comes into view, hurtling downward in close pursuit. Chris watches with his last breath, as the missile kisses the cargo planes nose, obliterating the cockpit. The plane explodes immediately, forcing Ben and James to take evasive action to avoid the debris. Chris is killed instantly, there was no surviving that blast and to Ben and James' knowledge, Emerson was also dead.

The UFO quickly vanishes off into the distance as both fighters' communications return. They watch in disbelief, as the devastated cargo plane plummets to the ground exploding again on impact. James is overwhelmed with shock, having fired the missile that had just killed his two fellow cadets, his friends. His best friend, Emerson was gone.

Chapter 7

It took a moment for Emerson to gather his thoughts. Was he dead? Where was he? Immediately after the light had presumably taken him, Emerson's life flashed before his eyes, like a movie playing backwards. Memorable moments of his past play out in front of him like a vivid dream. His vision becomes flooded with images of Chris moments earlier, Lana and the time they've spent. His late father appears and then the crash that took his life, Emerson's childhood right through to his mother holding him moments after birth before she passes. Then another flash of bright white light appears, this time it wasn't a memory. It is as though he is floating in the air, above himself laying on a gurney in an unfamiliar setting. This continues for what seems like a lifetime and each time the cycle passes, it gets faster and faster.

Eventually the replay starts to fade. Emerson slowly regains consciousness to hear the distant echo of a mechanical drone-like sound. It gets increasingly louder as he begins to wake from a deep, dream state. The slow, pulsating noise continues as Emerson begins to open his eyes. Not able to move, he stares up into a blinding white light that's fading dimmer than brightens with each pulse from the drone. As his eyes adjust, all he can see and hear is the pulsating light and sound, then darkness, over and over again. He begins to become agitated, still not able to move. As the light dims down to darkness, he feels a presence moving towards him. The light slowly comes back on, nothing could brace Emerson for what he was about to see. Looking directly down into his eyes, the silhouette of a face appeared. He couldn't quite make it out at first, but as the light gets brighter Emerson begins to realize that staring down was an extraterrestrial, humanoid creature. Instantly, he becomes petrified with fear. The creature is pale in complexion similar to a human, but thinner and ganglier. A larger head and huge eyes, black as the darkness of space, it was all too much for Emerson as he's overcome by fear. He can sense that the being meant no harm, although the reality of what he was witnessing was terrifying and confronting, like a thousand movies running through his mind at once. It raised its hand towards Emerson's face and he reacts by hyperventilating into unconsciousness within a matter of seconds.

Emerson, having witnessed something of an undisclosed nature aboard his plane, had now been transported onto some form of alien craft. His life on Earth compromised due to the content of the cargo the two men had accidentally seen. The next thing he can remember could only be described as a near death experience. He couldn't believe it was real, that it was actually happening.

Emerson has no idea how much time passed, but when he finally wakes he finds himself no longer on the craft, but lying on a circular stone floor inside a small tropical canyon. He's surrounded by crystal clear water with a single stone path leading to a cave.

Emerson takes a moment to try and make sense of what has happened. A million thoughts and immense confusion run through his head as he takes in the situation and beautiful new surroundings.

Back on Earth, news of the accident spreads quickly. James and Ben fly into Creech Air Force Base in the northern Mojave Desert. Within seconds of exiting the plane they are ushered into a holding room for immediate questioning.

The two commanding generals overseeing the mission arrive shortly after. James and Ben do their best to truthfully explain the details leading up to the incident. James was surprised in his own reaction to the Generals. It was though he expected their casual response. As though they already knew what had encountered their squad. Still visibly shaken due to believing he's responsible for the killing of two of his comrades, James eventually becomes impatient with the two Generals vague responses and queries them to reveal their knowledge of the UFO. He could tell they were withholding information to which James felt he was within his rights to know. The two generals quickly change their tone and shut James down in his attempt to push for answers. One of the generals stands abruptly out of his seat.

"What you both witnessed today is a tragedy, but also a matter of national security at the highest level. Extremely classified. Today's events can and will only be described as an unfortunate accident.

The extraterrestrial presence on earth has existed for thousands of years. Their intention is only to observe us without interfering with humanities natural course. Disclosure of an extraterrestrial existence would subsequently have a substantial effect on humanity's future, therefore you are both sworn to secrecy under the United States Military Disclosure Act. You are not to discuss any details of today's events with anyone under any circumstances. Not even each other. This never happened. Do you understand cadets!?"

The two men realizing the seriousness of the situation can only simultaneously reply; "Yes sir."

A world away, Emerson makes his way out of the canyon. He follows the path leading through a naturally carved stone tunnel to the top of a ridge. Sunlight hits his face where he sees this new world's horizon for the very first time. Any thought he had that was still somehow on earth quickly disappears with the incredible sight of a close orbiting planet on the horizon, filling half the scope of the sky. Emerson looks out over this immense unspoilt and untouched tropical oasis. He takes in the scenery for a moment, still trying to catch his thoughts and make sense of it all. He looks down from the ridge and through the thick foliage noticing what looks to be a path and begins to make his way down to it. As he follows the path, it becomes more obvious to him that the path was man made. Small carved steps and the odd footprint can be seen, although it doesn't look to have been used frequently. Emerson tentatively follows the path, unsure and weary of what he might encounter. As night falls, he ventures off the path to find a high and safe vantage point to build a secure shelter. It doesn't take long before he finds himself in a small clearing overlooking a large part of the domain. He gathered foliage and bark and created a makeshift shelter and bedding. His final thoughts before fading off into sleep; *'Where the hell am I?'*

On Earth, word of the incident had yet reached Lana. She was blissfully unaware as she places powder into the washing machine and sets the laundry in motion. As she places the washing powder back onto the shelf, she hears her cellphone. Walking back through her loft, Lana is unaware that on her television in the background, the news reporter is releasing the information on the devastating and explosive fiery crash. Photos of Chris & Emerson flash up on screen but Lana hadn't yet noticed. She answers the phone only to be told by the caller to turn on her television. She reaches for the remote and turns up the sound.

"No in-depth details have yet been released of this tragedy, however what is known is that the aircraft itself was a C-5 Galaxy military cargo plane. Early reports of the cause of the crash are leading towards mechanical failure. Though one eye witnesses has reported seeing the plane in a ball of flames plummeting to the ground. We do have the identities of the deceased pilots; Cadets Chris Lund and Emerson Ryles. Both were stationed at Moody Air Force Base in Georgia, apparently in their last months of training. Sadly, both young men have been killed and families are being notified as we bring this story to you. We will give you more updates on this breaking story as it comes in. Now in other news..."

Lana drops the phone from her ear and brings her hands to her face as her world is instantly turned upside down. She gasps and begins sobbing at the sight of Emerson's face smiling back at her on the screen. She stumbles to the couch and sits, overcome by emotion as images of the wreckage are broadcast all throughout the country, playing over and over. In a cruel twist, after finally been reunited with her soul mate for little more than a week, Lana bursts into uncontrollable cries as she realizes she has lost Emerson for a second time.

Chapter 8

Tens of thousands of light years away in another Galaxy, Emerson makes it through his first night. He wakes early from a restless night's sleep, hoping somehow this had all been an extremely bad dream. He looks out over the horizon to an oasis of untouched rain forests, rivers and the welcoming sight of an ocean on the horizon. Lights of what looked to be a small camp fire could be seen earlier in the night in the direction of the ocean. Emerson decided to make his way back down the ridge and continue on the track towards where he believed the fire would have been.

Hunger and thirst begin to set in as Emerson continued his trek for a few more hours. Finally, he reaches a small water hole and stops briefly for a drink and to rest. The beautiful surroundings were so pristine and peaceful and Emerson had become to marvel in these unfamiliar surroundings. While still feeling unending fear and confusion, he felt it could have been far worse than resting by a crystal clear spring and the tropical paradise around it.

Suddenly, the silence and tranquility of the beautiful surroundings were abruptly interrupted by the distant sound of an oncoming voice in the wind. Emerson quickly swung around and kept low as he focused in on the sound and where it was coming from. As it got closer, the unmistakable noise could be recognized as a person singing. Emerson quickly hid himself from view as the melody kept getting closer and closer. Emerson found a place to hide among some bushes near the spring and waited.

All of a sudden, from the far side of the waterhole appeared an old man. He was human; at least Emerson thought he looked human. The man appeared to be in his seventies and was standing less than thirty feet away. Emerson slowly maneuvered himself to get a better look at the old man's face. The old man hears the rustling and is startled quickly turning in Emerson's direction.

"Come on boy. No use in hiding now," the man instructed.

Emerson stepped out into view as the man peers into the bushes. The man spoke perfect English which gave Emerson a sense of comfort. The man looked him up and down, instantly recognising Emerson as a pilot by his uniform. He enthusiastically walked towards Emerson who carefully looked around for an exit strategy, just in case.

"A pilot, huh? Oh, it's so good to see you boy. It's been such a long time since I've seen someone from home. My name's Tuk."

Tuk extends his hand in friendship and tentatively Emerson returns the gesture.

"Emerson. My name is Emerson. Where the hell am I?"

"So what year is it back home? Oh, you have bought back some good memories. Who is the president? What part of the states you from boy?"

Emerson had his own questions but couldn't get a word in over the excited old man, and his inquisitive random questions about Earth. Tuk was obviously surprised to see him and fascinated to hear the latest developments back on Earth. He divulges to Emerson that he was abducted in the mid-forties, though he hadn't seen another abductee for some time.

"You kind of lose sense of time here. I know it's been around thirty or forty years, but after a while you stop keeping count and resign to it."

A sense of doom had overcome Emerson as he listened to Tuk subtly convince him to also resign to the fact that this was his new home.

"Come on boy. Best take you to the village. Are they going to be shocked to see you!"

Silently, Emerson followed the old man back to the path and along the way he tells him all about the ways of his new world.

"I don't know why they took me. I was a pilot myself you know."

"Really? For the military?"

"I was boy. It seems so long ago now, it was 1945. We took off from Ft Lauderdale, Florida, just on a routine training mission. Not long into the flight our navigational equipment went haywire, then before we knew it we were running low on fuel. The next thing, we're all in a panic preparing to ditch in the ocean, suddenly a flash of light, BAM ... snatched me up ... then I woke up here ... that was nearly 35 years ago," Tuk reminisced.

"35 years? It's 2014 on Earth, Tuk. That was 69 years ago. So you were a pilot of flight 19?" Emerson exclaimed puzzled.

"Flight 19 ... ahhh, that's right boy... 14 of us went down."

Tuk now had more questions than ever; Emerson could barely ask any of his own as they both made their way back to Tuks village.

The trek was long as Tuk was quite slow and easily distracted. They spent some time talking about each other's past before they arrived at the village. The inhabitants of the village were surprised and intrigued by the outsider's presence. They approached Emerson with tenderness and care welcoming him. Emerson felt comfortable and as he looked around he noticed that the village consisted of an assortment of humans living as though they were from ancient times. No modern buildings or steel structures could be seen, but dwellings of magnificent stone architecture and strong wooden houses dotted the village landscape. Most of the people were of a tribal nature and spoke in an ancient language. As Emerson focused on what they were saying he recognized the language, or at least parts of it. He remembers back to linguistics training and recalls the brief moment they passed over the evolution of language from the ancient Mayan culture. There were others amongst the villagers who spoke both the archaic Mayan dialect and English.

It was amazing and a little overwhelming how peaceful Emerson was finding his new home and how easily he was settling in. The obvious familiarity of man helped but also the release of fear. He felt no conflict here, no aggression. There was this peace that floated through the air, through the stream current, through the trees and through each individual he spoke with. It was utopia.

Emerson and Tuk become close friends. They had an uncanny amount in common and Tuk was always intrigued and grateful to hear of modern day aircraft capabilities and stories alike. Emerson often felt that he was recalling flashbacks of his father when he spoke to Tuk. Tuk's personality and character were similar in a way to the memories of his father. Maybe that was why over time they bonded so well.

Chapter 9

While Emerson embraced his new life and new world, back on Earth things were not so serene. Ben, James, Lana, friends, family & comrades of Chris and Emerson gathered to farewell the two men in a full military service memorial.

Lana arrived at the service still distraught and in disbelief that Emerson was gone. Such a cruel twist, to be reunited after ten years only to be stolen away again so soon. Lana finds it all too much to take in and breaks into tears. Both James and Chris stand either side of her consoling and embracing her. The 21-gun salute rains out over the cemetery followed by the mighty roar of four military jets performing the 'missing man fly over'. Later at the wake, Lana brings herself to ask Ben and James about the incident.

"I don't know how to deal with this. Maybe if I knew what happened I can come to terms with it?"

"I know Lana. It's hard for us to make sense of ourselves. It was an accident. A malfunction. That's all I can tell you," James answered, knowingly lying.

Ben and James look at each other with regret. They couldn't disclose any information of what they really saw and what difference would it make if they could? Emerson and Chris were gone either way. The pain would still be real for them and for Lana. They were just as shaken by the loss, especially James.

A month later, James dropped out of the Air Force overcome with the grief of the events and circumstances of that fateful day. Ben continued flying, putting the matter behind him and joining with another squadron. Eventually over time, Lana slowly began to pick herself up and she began writing songs again with support from friends and family, eventually continuing on singing and finding inspiration from her memory of Emerson. In fact it was textbook, most went on with their life. They grieved their loss, mourned their friend and tried to move on. James suffered more than most as he retreated into a bottle of whiskey near daily, but nothing really unusual developed for anyone. The military could lock their secret up under the fake pretense they had created and also move on, at least for now.

A few months passed and Emerson had become accustomed to his new life and surroundings. An ionisation phase ensues over time with regular tribal rituals of hunting dangerous unique predators in the jungles under the effects of a unique and traditional hallucinogenic drink. He became accepted among the young tribal warriors, providing for the people and becoming a respected member of the community. Life seemed to be going well, Emerson could almost see himself living out his days happily on the new planet if only he hadn't a burning desire to be reunited with Lana.

Over time, Emerson created the reasoning for this world and its return to an ancient culture. With his home planet in a state of disarray it made sense that if there were peaceful beings elsewhere in the galaxy that they may want to give mankind a second chance and rebuild from scratch. The relationships he had formed on his new home had shown him he had been selected amongst a very defined and intriguing group of people. Maybe it was a rebirth of mankind; the true Eden. Many evenings were spent in deep conversation on all manner of things with Tuk. Amazing tales of the past often left Emerson in awe, as Tuk was a brilliant story teller and character. As close to a father figure Emerson had had for some time.

One evening during another deep conversation, Emerson expressed his desire to return to Earth and to Lana. Tuk also had family when he was abducted and longed to return for many years. However he explained to Emerson how he was deemed too much of a liability to be returned to Earth having witnessed and seen far too much. This was new information for Emerson as they had never discussed any chance of return before. Emerson became intrigued and inquisitive to this new found news and possibility.

"What do you mean deemed a liability? Who made that call? Can we actually go back?" queried Emerson.

"Settle down boy. You have next to no chance and it's been years since the council granted this to anyone," replied Tuk.

"Really! Who was that?"

"Michelson? Yeah, an old professor from Oxford University was granted return. I'm not sure exactly why they let him go back, but most likely he is a slave to the military," explained Tuk.

"No offence Tuk, but I really don't care about some professor. How can I get back? What do I have to do?" demanded Emerson.

"Well, remember the circular stone platform you arrived on when you first arrived here?"

"Yeah?"

"OK, so you need to go there and about another 10 miles west you come to a huge stone building with a massive dome roof. That's the council lodging. You can only ever get one request for a hearing from the council. They will grant the hearing but I don't think they will say yes."

"Why not?" Emerson was tiring to all the blocks Tuk was putting forward.

"Like I said, it's not taken lightly and only once, that I know of, has it been granted before and the reasons were very circumstantial. I don't want you getting your hopes up boy"

"Let's go." Emerson insisted.

Emerson headed straight to his dwelling and began gathering the few small possessions he had and prepared to leave. When he walked back out, Tuk was standing there with a knapsack over his shoulder. Even though Tuk said there was little chance in Emerson's desire to go back being granted, the natural instinct of everyone was to pass on their hope and best wishes as word spread quickly that he was preparing to leave. Such a natural and kind culture that he had been a part of. Emerson felt confident he would get home, but a part of him realized what a great place he would be leaving.

Tuk and a few others joined Emerson on the three day trek back to the platform and then onto the dome. For the majority of the time they travelled in silence, Emerson reflected on Lana and the glimmer of hope he had been given. How strong his love had become over the months apart. It was a testament to their connection. He thought to himself how his feelings had not faded but grown.

Finally, after a three day trek, they had arrived. An obscure, tall domed stone building built awkwardly into the side of a cliff face awaited them. Tuk had not seen this place for nearly 68 years. Memories of the day he was denied to return to his own family came flooding back, as did the memory of his family.

Tuk turned to his fellow villagers and thanked them for accompanying them. One by one they acknowledged Emerson before heading back to the village.

"Aren't you going to go too?" asked Emerson.

"What? And leave all the excitement for you? Doubt it boy," replied Tuk, jokingly patting his friend on the back. "Come on son. We've come this far, let's go in."

They traversed the seemingly endless number of stairs and entered the alien dwelling. Seeing the beings faces again was still as confronting and terrifying for Emerson as it was the first time he saw them. Reminding himself of his mission, he put aside all fear. He knew the next few moments would determine his fate for the rest of his life. Both men hear and recognize the unmistakable pulsating droning sound resonate through the chamber as the beings commander and what appeared to be a military General are flown in. They disembark the craft making their way into the chamber and to their seats. Emerson is dumbfounded to see a human in full military uniform sit side by side with the beings.

"Hello Tuk, you've aged well," said the General.

"Morning," replied the jovial Tuk.

"Not trying again are we?" he asked Tuk.

"Not me sir. No. Young Emerson here wants to plead his case. I told him there would be no chance, but..."

The General rudely cut him off, "Emerson. You are not happy here? You have no close family on Earth"

"Define happiness, General."

"No war, no loss, no grief, no famine, what you have been living within the last six months. Has this not been a pleasant environment for you?"

"This is a utopia General, but no I am not happy here. I trained my entire life to become a military pilot for the United States Air Force. I wish to return to this life. I feel it was unfair that I was abducted having accidently witnessed the contents aboard my plane. I have a life on Earth."

The General went to speak but the alien being next to him raised its hand to stop the General. He titled his head and peered into Emerson's mind, his soul. The being stared into Emerson's eyes intensely as though their two minds became interconnected. It could feel the emptiness, and burning desire he desperately needed to return. The being could see Emerson's kind nature and good intentions that his character was attributed to.

The being stood and walked towards Emerson. Emerson nervously stood his ground. So much taller in stature than an average human, yet there was serenity about the being that took away the anxiety Emerson was feeling. The being stared intensively into

Emerson eyes as though looking deeper into his mind and thoughts.

He then turned and made his way back to his seat. He looked to the General and telepathically relayed a decision to him. The General was visibly taken back to what he was being told which raised Tuk's curiosity. He whispered to Emerson, "This is strange. The General looks concerned."

"The council has made its decision," the General said in a stern and defining tone, "It is true that it was not your fault that you became aware of the contents aboard your plane. Once you became aware, there was no other choice but to do what we had to keep the secrets of this existence safe, hence rendering your abduction a necessity."

"Then why was Chris not taken also?"

The alien raised its hand again stopping the General. This time he peered back at Emerson and communicated.

"What happened to your comrade was unfortunate but not of our doing. We rebuild civilizations in preparation for what will come. We do so with minds and hearts of the pure. This does not exclude the reckless but it does

make them unsuitable for relocation. Your friend met his peace with no pain, no suffering. He is home, he walks freely within the brightness. The same brightness you came through. He is at rest."

Emerson nodded with acceptance to the beings unique and genuine explanation.

The General continued.

"You will be given a similar alternative that was granted to the pilots of the F-18s. They've both been instructed what many men before them have been told. That the things they have witnessed cannot be comprehended by family or loved ones or anyone in the general population. Hence as a matter of national security disclosure of any information you are now aware of carries severe consequences. You will never return here. You can never talk of this place or what you saw on the day you were abducted. You cannot contact anyone. You have been granted return status on the basis for you to begin a new life serving as a special class air force pilot. But understand it will not be as Emerson Ryles. Emerson Ryles died in a plane crash. You must start a new life and never attempt to contact anyone you knew previously."

Emerson hid his true thoughts as well as he could, but something inside him knew that the alien being knew exactly what he was thinking. How could they let him go back, knowing he would defy everything the General had just said? Wouldn't the being know that this was his intention? Regardless, Emerson nodded in agreement. If the being did know, the General certainly didn't. If Emerson's obvious intention to find Lana became known to him, he would never be going back.

"I will reiterate to you that any breach of these terms will result in your likely death and of those you have put at risk. Do you understand this?" the General enforced.

Again, Emerson nodded in acceptance.

Just then two armed guards entered the chamber from the waiting craft. The General addressed them all bringing the meeting to a close.

"Emerson Ryles you have been granted return status. I don't believe I need to repeat how severely you will suffer if any word of your experience here or surrounding it is uttered. You will now be guided to a waiting transport that will take us back to Earth where you will begin your new life."

As the General was talking, Emerson turned to Tuk and thought to himself if there was ever a chance for him it would be now.

"Excuse me sir," he interrupted, "I wish to thank you for your decision and graciously ask from the council to grant return status to Tuk."

The General didn't entertain the thought for a second and closed the hearing. As the General left, he stared at Emerson knowing he had done him a great favor and felt confident that he wouldn't become a problem.

Emerson turned to Tuk, "Sorry, my friend, I tried."

Tuk smiles and embraced his dear friend with pride. Emerson returns the show of friendship.

"Thank you Tuk, you've been a great friend. I wish you were coming back."

"Ahh this is my home now boy," Tuk replies, hiding his disappointment but relief for Emerson.

"You've been like a father to me Tuk. I'll never forget you."

Tuk wishes Emerson all the best as he slips a secret note for his family into his jacket. He had prepared it earlier in case of this outcome. Emerson quickly tucks it away.

"All good boy. Live a full life. One John would have been proud of."

Emerson nodded and followed the others to the transport. As he headed up the stairs to the roof of the dome, suddenly Emerson clicked and stopped. He turned, but it was too late, Tuk had gone. He realized that he had never told Tuk his father's name, yet Tuk knew it. He thought to himself with a smile; *"You certainly are one of a kind my friend. Too few of a kind"*

With that the four men and two beings boarded the waiting craft and got underway journeying back home, to Earth.

Chapter 18

The journey back was remarkably quick. Emerson walked about the craft admiring the profoundly advanced engineering and technology. The fighter jets he was used to seemed primitive in comparison. No longer than an hour had passed, before they were re-entering the Earth's atmosphere. Near the front of the ship sat two of the beings and the General from the council. One of the beings began talking telepathically with the General. It informed him of Emerson's true intention to contact people from his previous life back on Earth. The General acknowledges the beings and assures them that it will be taken care off.

The craft transports the four men onto the tarmac under the cover of darkness just outside a hanger near Area 51. Just as quickly as it arrived, the craft disappeared into the night sky. The four men walked towards the giant hanger where armed guards stood on either side of the massive entrance. Three F-22 fighters sat lined up outside the hanger along with a few military jeeps. The men walked in through the massive roller door and it began to shut behind them. Emerson could sense something wasn't quite right, if something seems too good to be true it usually is. He asked where they're going. The General turns to Emerson as they're walking. In a demeaning tone he answered,

"I'm not going to lie to you cadet, I don't trust you. I'm not as naive as our extraterrestrial friends and I don't think for one minute that you won't try return to your old life. We are heading down to the main lab where you'll be implanted with a tracking device and monitored for the rest of your life. If you as so much think about contacting people you previously knew, I will put a bullet into your skull myself."

The General continued down the walkway. Emerson stopped. A sensation of dread runs through his body. The slow moving roller door is seven feet off the ground. At that moment he realized he may never see Lana again. He looked back at the closing roller door then suddenly sprinted towards it. The two guards were slow to react and the General screamed at them.

"Stop him! Now! Shoot him!"

As Emerson slid under the door the guards' machine gun fire showers bullets everywhere. The door closed behind him. Emerson jumps up and sprints towards one of the F-22's. He leaps onto the wing just as alarms in the hanger start whaling. He pulls the cockpit door down and listens to 1100 horse power of jet turbine engine wind up. He can see jeeps in the distance bearing down on him as he punches the throttle full forward. A lone jeep parked in line of the thrust hurtles through the air, cartwheeling across the tarmac and smashed into the side of the hanger. Within seconds, Emerson is in the air.

He flies south-east avoiding any nearby military air bases and headed for the city of New Orleans. This is where he believed James might still be living. After flying at 1500mph he's now only 100 miles from the city. Emerson brings the plane down to 5000 feet,

300mph and pulls hard up on the stick, punching the throttle flat then ejects from the plane, sending the jet up into the upper stratosphere.

Emerson braced himself as his parachute opened and coasted down to land, scoping out the nearest rural house south of Baton Rouge.

Once on the ground he spotted a small farm house only a few hundred yards away and quickly made his way towards it. Emerson arrived at the front porch of the house. A weary middle age couple come to the front door. Emerson, luckily wearing military attire, convinced the couple he'd gotten lost and had simply run out of fuel. The couple graciously invited him in to use their phone where he considered calling Lana, but instead called James, hoping he's not far.

James has just poured himself his third whiskey of the evening and stood on his balcony of the small one bedroom loft, looking down over the evening lights of New Orleans. He turns and heads back in as the phone rings.

"Yeah?" he answered.

When James hears Emerson's voice he freezes, shocked in utter disbelief.

"I can't talk for long. They could be listening in on us. Where are you James?" Emerson spluttered.

Luckily for Emerson, James was less than an hour away. He gave James the farm house address, reminded him to be alert of who may be around and hung up the phone. Emerson very politely thanked the old couple again for their generosity. They graciously offer him a cup of tea which Emerson accepts with a smile and fitting with the charade, struck up small talk while waiting for James.

Forty five minutes passed, when the unmistakable roar of a V8 muscle car came speeding up the driveway, screeching to a halt. James stepped out of the vehicle, freezing suddenly as he comes face to face with a ghost. He couldn't believe Emerson was standing right there in front of him. The two comrades walk towards one another. James embraces his mate in disbelief, tearing up.

"I thought I'd bloody killed you. How are you here?" he asks.

"I'll let you know everything on the way. You won't believe a word of it." Emerson replied.

As the two men jumped into the car, Emerson thanked the old couple for their hospitality. They both have confused looks on their faces to the conversation they just witnessed, but smiled and waved them off.

Emerson filled James in on the entire unbelievable story as they're driving back towards the city, and his need to find Lana. James hadn't been able to bring himself to speak with Lana since the funeral. He also mentioned how he had dropped out of the Air Force not long after the incident and Ben was assigned to a new squad.

Emerson and James made it back to James' apartment. They made their way through the building, assuring not to make contact or be seen by anyone. Emerson closed the door to James' apartment, "This place has seen better days" Emerson mentions.

"Yeah well, I would have tidied up if I knew you were going to fall from the sky," James jokes. "I could look online and see if

Lana's touring again. I did know she went back into the studio a few months ago."

"No, not online, not here. We can't leave any trail."

James rumbles through one of his drawers and eventually pulls out an old cell phone of an ex-girlfriend.

"Bingo," he exclaimed and started searching online for information on Lana. Sure enough, it didn't take long until they found some dates, the next being in three days time in Denver, Colorado. James and Emerson waste no time, knowing military personnel won't be far behind. They wait until early in the morning and stealthily leave the apartment building. James stored his car at a parking garage a few blocks away. Once there, they hit the road seemingly undetected, driving 16 hours straight, and only stopping for fuel. The two men felt confident, yet wary, they could get to Colorado undetected.

Emerson considered calling Lana but edged on the side of caution, just in case they don't make it. Along the way, James listens in awe as Emerson recounts his experiences of the past six months another world away. He tells of Tuk and shows James Tuks letter to his wife. The two men realize the seriousness of the truths they both now know. James however seems mostly unconcerned, just relived that Emerson is still alive. After two days of solid driving they finally make it across the Colorado border traversing the scenic mountainous interstate 70.

They're less than a day away from Denver making good time for Lana's next performance. James and Emerson pull up at a small service station at the top of a scenic mountain range. Emerson goes into pay for fuel as James fills up the car. Everything is quiet and still as James looks out over the range, admiring the view which seemed to go on forever. Suddenly the tranquil peacefulness of the canyon is interrupted, as the distinctive sound of a helicopter can be heard beyond the horizon. Emerson also noticed the sound on the wind from inside the gas station. They both look at one another. As James turns back around, an Apache helicopter comes up out of the ridge pointing straight at the car. James throws the fuel pump away and jumps into the car speeding off with a violent roar and leaving two black lines and a cloud of smoke down the highway. The apache tilts forward hard in close pursuit. Emerson runs out to see James speeding off, drawing the Apache after him and away from the gas station. Emerson watches helplessly as he can see James trying to escape, but the car is no real match for the Apache. Less than a quarter mile down the road .50 caliber bullets start tearing up the road around him. James comes up to a large sweeping bend where the Apache lines him up and fires again fragmenting the car. James takes a direct hit. Emerson stands helpless as he watches James smash through the guard rail and plummet end over end a few hundred feet down the mountain side finally coming to rest and exploding into flames at the bottom of a ravine. Emerson can't believe his eyes. He has to think quickly and heads into the bathroom in the side of the service station to keep out of sight. He stands in front of the grimy old mirror processing what he just witnessed. James sacrificed himself without question. Emerson could still hear the Apache. He peers through the window louvers. Satisfied with the resulting carnage, the

Apache retreats into the distance, leaving the burning wreckage to the elements.

Chapter 11

Emerson, in absolute shock, exits the rest room. Deciding to keep away from the road, he walks around the side of the gas station and spots a road bike parked up against a wall. He has no option but to steal it and get as far as possible before police and alike arrive on the scene. He pushes the bike away from the wall far enough to start it up without notice. Onlookers begin to gather out on the main road heading towards the fiery wreckage that was his best friend. No one takes any notice as he starts up the bike and speeds off continuing for Denver.

By pure luck, with throttle wide open, Emerson makes it to Denver without further incident. Still grieving and in shock from James' sacrifice, Emerson finds a quite inner-city motel. He pays with cash from a few dollars James had prepared for him. Emerson hides the bike from both road and air view under a carport next to an old F-truck. He heads to the room.

Emerson hurriedly stumbles through the front door peering through the dusty window ensuring he hadn't been followed. Satisfied he's secure he pulls the green, musky curtains closed, leans against the wall next to the window and examines the grimy cheap motel room he had just entered. An empty side table sits on the eastern wall and above, an old television loosely hangs from its brackets. A dirty brown mat leads into a tiny bathroom he had yet to encounter. Barely a double bed presses up against the opposite wall with a tired and battered bed side table struggling to hold up the phone. He lets out an exhausting sign and lunges forward slumping onto the bed.

Emerson's thoughts wander back to his friend James. Still in disbelief he places his hands over his head and attempts to snap himself out of the overwhelming emotion. He takes a look at his watch and is relieved to see he has six hours before Lana's show. He falls exhausted and restless onto the bed staring up at the cigarette stained ceiling, Emerson thoughts wander back to the memory of his Father. How much he wished for his advice, his council, if just a single reassuring thought. Whether it was a conscious thought or the beginning of a dream, Emerson's mind slips back in time, to a simpler place. His old home town of Anamosa, Iowa. As his consciousness slips away he falls off into an exhausted deep sleep.

Emerson wakes realizing he's over an hour late and has possibly missed Lana's show. He hurriedly gets his things together and rides into the city. He leaves the bike in an alley across from the venue and makes his way into the bar, constantly checking for suspicious people and movements.

Emerson walks through the front doors and works his way through the crowd. As he looks up onto the stage everything feels as though it is in slow motion. The most beautiful, amazing woman, whom he thought for a long time he'd never see again, has gone from being a world away to finally just feet. The emotion in Lana's voice cuts deep into the entire crowd. Emerson still grieving from watching James being killed does well to keep himself together.

He walks through to the center of the crowd, mesmerized and so proud of seeing his Lana perform with such soul. He can only imagine what she must have gone through having believed he had died. Every night he had wished he could have just let her know that he was OK. Lana stands at the front of the stage, microphone in hand. Emerson stands back from the stage, mixed into the crowd taking in the moment. As Lana's set is almost over she looks out into the crowd, somehow out of all the people in the building, she manages to spot Emerson. They lock eyes and are both frozen in time. Lana nearly drops the microphone staring at her soul mate with a look of shock and disbelief on her face. She jumps down from the stage making her way quickly through the crowd. She throws herself into Emerson's arms and bursts into tears. She can't believe it, having to take a second look at him just to make sure. Lana feels so confused, yet overwhelmed with joy. Emerson holds her tight. The crowd seems confused at first but as the reunited couple kiss and embrace, they all begin to cheer and applaud.

Emerson and Lana leave Denver that night and a few days later the two cross the border into Mexico. Emerson eventually stays true to his word, tracking down Tuk's wife. She receives the mysterious letter in the mail. The letter Tuk had slipped into Emerson's jacket a world away. It explained his disappearance and regret he couldn't be there. Wishing his family all the best and not to worry. Finally, after 69 years Tuk's wife, now in her late 90s, knows the truth and finds some happiness in knowing he's alive, she finally feels a sense of closure.

Emerson and Lana changed their names and moved to a small beach front town in Salina Cruz, Mexico. Ever mindful that one day the military will surely figure out he's still alive and where they are. The secrets and truths Emerson now knew, had given the couple a certain death sentence, if caught. The thought and consequences seemed diminished though, in each others company. Emerson and Lana had seemed to have found their happy ending, for now anyway. The kindness and humanity of the world away awoke a part of Emerson that he had forgotten since his father had passed. He reflected, hand in hand, as he walked the beach with his beautiful Lana, forever grateful and indebted to those who gave their all with nothing in it for them; Chris, Tuk and James. Forever grateful for their friendship and selfless sacrifice, forever indebted to live on in their memory and make sure their lives' influence would not be lost in vein. With the couples new found knowledge of the wonders of the universe around them, the world that they knew would never look the same. Every day Emerson would think of James. How James' fate was meant to be his own. The world had a right to know the truth. Though for now, keeping a low profile and protecting the women of his dreams was his number one priority. As long as the military heads thought Emerson was no longer alive, there was a chance to unlock the secrets from within. Like a ghost in the night the pieces of the puzzle will begin to appear. If the secret service tries closing in, all bets are off. Mass disclosure will become unstoppable. An awakening of the most profound secret ever kept in human history would become common knowledge for humanities greater good. The dawn of a new age, lies in the hands of the forgotten.

To be continued..............

9159241R00060

Made in the USA
San Bernardino, CA
06 March 2014